CARTER HIGH
MYSTERIES

THE FIELD TRIP

Mystery

By Eleanor Robins

SADDLEBACK
EDUCATIONAL PUBLISHING

CARTER HIGH
M Y S T E R I E S

SADDLEBACK
EDUCATIONAL PUBLISHING
www.sdlback.com

ISBN-13: 978-1-61651-563-8
ISBN-10: 1-61651-563-5
eBook: 978-1-61247-131-0

Printed in Guangzhou, China
0112/CA21200062

16 15 14 13 12   2 3 4 5 6 7

Chapter 1

Drake was at school. He was in the hall. He was on his way to his science class. His friend, Jack, was with him.

Drake said, "I didn't have time to do my science homework. So I hope Mr. Zane doesn't give us a surprise test today, dude."

"I hope the same. That's for sure," Jack said.

Both boys had Mr. Zane for science. But not at the same time.

"But Mr. Zane might give us a surprise test. He hasn't given us one in a while. And it's about time for him to do that," Drake said.

Drake got to Mr. Zane's room.

He said, "See you later, Jack."

"Bye," Jack said.

Jack went on down the hall. And Drake went into his classroom.

The bell rang to start class.

Mr. Zane called the roll.

Then Mr. Zane said, "Now we'll talk about our field trip."

"What field trip?" Noah asked. Noah sat next to Drake.

"You should raise your hand when you wish to speak," Mr. Zane said.

Noah raised his hand.

"What field trip?" Noah asked again.

Drake hoped it was to somewhere he wanted to go. But he had a feeling it wouldn't be.

"We'll go on a trip to Bartow Gardens," Mr. Zane said.

"When are we going?" Drake asked.

Drake was on the football team. He hoped the trip wasn't on a day when he had a game.

Mr. Zane said, "We'll go next Friday. Tomorrow I'll give you a permission slip to take home. You must have a parent sign it. And you must return it to me by this Friday."

"What if we don't want to go?" Noah asked.

Drake had a game that night. And he didn't want to go on the trip. But he would never tell Mr. Zane that.

Mr. Zane didn't seem pleased.

"All students will go on the field trip," Mr. Zane said.

"But what if a student isn't here that day?" Noah asked.

"Then the student must bring a note from a doctor," Mr. Zane said.

Noah said, "My parents don't have a

lot of money. So I can't pay to go on the field trip. So I guess I can't go."

That surprised Drake. Noah always had a lot of money. Drake was sure Noah could pay to go on the field trip. So why did Noah say that?

Mr. Zane said, "Students don't need to worry about money. The school will pay for the field trip. Students won't have to pay anything."

Noah didn't seem happy to hear that. But Drake was glad to hear it.

Drake was sure Noah didn't want to go on the trip. And Drake didn't want to go on the day of a game.

But Drake knew that didn't matter. Mr. Zane wanted them to go. So they would have to go.

Mr. Zane didn't give them a surprise test. But Drake was still glad when his science class was over.

Drake hurried out into the hall. Jack came over to him. So did their friend, Logan. All three boys lived at Grayson Apartments.

Jack asked, "What did you do in science class today? Did you have a surprise test?"

"Yeah. Did you have a surprise test?" Logan asked.

Jack and Logan had Mr. Zane for science, too.

"No. Mr. Zane said all of his classes are going on a field trip. And he talked a lot about the field trip," Drake said.

"Where are we going?" Logan asked.

"We're going to Bartow Gardens. Some people will talk to us about the flowers," Drake said.

"That doesn't sound like much fun. Do we all have to go?" Logan asked.

"Yeah, Mr. Zane said all students

have to go. Or we need a doctor's note," Drake said.

Logan said, "It had better be a note from a real doctor. Because Mr. Zane will call. And he'll find the truth."

"That's for sure," Jack said.

Drake was sure Mr. Zane would do that, too.

"Maybe the trip won't be so bad," Logan said.

Drake said, "But I have a game that night. And I don't want to go on a field trip that day."

Jack said, "I need to go to class. I'll see you at lunch. But I'll be late. I have to stop by the library."

Jack hurried down the hall.

The first bell rang.

Logan said, "I need to get to class. I have Mr. Zane next. And you know I can't be late to his class."

"Yeah. See you at lunch," Drake said.

"I won't see you at lunch. I'm eating with someone," Logan said.

Then Logan hurried into his classroom.

Drake knew that Logan was eating lunch with a girl. Logan liked to date many girls. And some days Logan ate lunch with one of his girlfriends.

Chapter 2

Later that day, Drake walked into the lunchroom. Logan hurried over to him.

Logan said, "Don't forget, Drake. I'm eating with someone. So don't come over to my table."

"I won't forget," Drake said.

Logan quickly got his lunch. Then he went to a table and sat down.

Drake got his lunch. Then he looked for Jack. He didn't see Jack. But Jack said he would be late.

Then Drake saw Paige, Lin, and Willow. Drake went over to their table. He sat down.

Paige asked, "Is Logan eating by himself today?"

"No. A girl is going to eat with him," Drake said.

"Who?" Paige asked.

"I don't know. He didn't say," Drake said.

"Where's Jack? Is he eating with a girl, too?" Paige asked.

Drake said, "No, he's just late to lunch. He had to go to the library before lunch."

"Why?" Paige asked.

"I don't know. He didn't say why," Drake said.

Drake thought Paige asked too many questions about Logan and Jack. And he was glad when Willow said something.

Willow said, "I heard Mr. Zane's classes are going on a field trip."

Willow had Mr. Zane, too. But she had Mr. Zane after lunch.

"Yeah, we're going on a field trip," Drake said. But he didn't sound happy about it.

"Where are you going?" Lin asked.

"Yes. Tell us about it," Paige said.

"We're going to Bartow Gardens. We're going to learn about flowers," Drake said.

"That sounds like fun," Lin said.

"I think it does, too," Paige said.

"I wish I could go," Lin said.

"So do I," Paige said.

Lin and Paige didn't have Mr. Zane for science. So they wouldn't go.

"I wish you could go. And I could stay here," Drake said.

"Why?" Paige asked.

"Yes, why? I want to go," Willow said.

"I don't want to listen to someone talk about flowers," Drake said.

"I would like to hear about flowers," Lin said.

"So would I. What about you, Willow?" Paige asked.

"I think it'll be fun to go on the trip. And I want to learn about flowers, too," Willow said.

"I'm glad you three would like to hear about flowers. But I have to play football that night. And you don't. So I want to stay at school that day," Drake said.

"Why?" Paige asked.

"I don't want to walk around gardens all day. I'll get tired before the game," Drake said.

"So don't go on the trip. Tell Mr. Zane you'll stay here. And you'll write a paper about flowers. Or about something else," Paige said.

"I have to go. Mr. Zane said all students have to go. Unless they bring a note from a doctor," Drake said.

"Too bad, Drake. You'll just have to go

on the trip. And try to like it," Paige said.

"Yes, you will," Willow said.

Drake knew Paige and Willow were right. He did have to try to like the trip. But Drake didn't think he would.

And he wished he could think of a way to stay at school. Then he wouldn't have to go on the trip.

Chapter 3

It was the next morning. Drake was on his way to his science class. Logan and Jack were with him.

Drake said, "Maybe Mr. Zane has changed his mind. And maybe we won't have to go on the field trip."

Logan said, "No way. Mr. Zane said we're going. And he won't change his mind about that."

"That's for sure," Jack said.

"But I can hope he will," Drake said.

"Yeah," said Logan. "But hope is all you can do."

"Maybe the trip won't be so bad. Maybe

we can sit together on the bus. And then walk around the gardens together," Drake said.

"No way! Mr. Zane will make us stay with our own class," Logan said.

"That's for sure," Jack said.

"Yeah," Drake said. "You're right. He will."

Drake got to Mr. Zane's room. He said, "See you later." Then Drake went into his classroom.

Mr. Zane was walking around the room. He seemed upset.

Drake quickly walked over to his desk and sat down.

Noah came into class. He sat down next to Drake.

Drake said, "Mr. Zane seems upset, dude. Do you know why he's upset?"

"Why would I know? I didn't do anything wrong," Noah said.

"I didn't say you did. But I thought you might know," Drake said.

"Well, I don't," Noah said.

The bell rang to start class.

Mr. Zane called the roll.

Then Noah asked, "Mr. Zane, when will we get the permission slips?"

Drake didn't know why Noah asked Mr. Zane that question. Drake wasn't in a hurry to get his permission slip. And he didn't think Noah was in a hurry to get his permission slip either. So why did Noah ask Mr. Zane that?

But maybe Noah had thought about the field trip. And maybe he wanted to go now.

Mr. Zane looked at Noah.

Mr. Zane said, "You should raise your hand when you wish to speak."

Noah raised his hand.

Then Noah asked, "When will we get

the permission slips? I want to put mine into my backpack. So I won't forget to take it home," Noah said.

"All of you must come by my room after school. And you can get your permission slips then," Mr. Zane said.

"Why can't we get them now, Mr. Zane?" Noah asked.

Drake said, "I can't come by your room after school, Mr. Zane. I have to go to football practice as soon as school is over. And I don't have time to come by your room."

Mr. Zane looked at Drake. And he didn't seem pleased.

Drake wished he hadn't said that to Mr. Zane. He didn't mean to say it. It just slipped out.

Mr. Zane said, "Something has happened to the permission slips. I put them on my desk. And now they're missing."

"How can they be missing, Mr. Zane?" Noah asked.

Drake wanted to know that, too.

Mr. Zane said, "I don't know how they can be missing. But they are. And I'll have to run off some more during my lunch."

"Can we get the permission slips tomorrow?" Noah asked.

Drake was glad Noah asked that. Drake wanted to know the answer, too. But he wouldn't dare ask Mr. Zane that.

Mr. Zane said, "All students must come to my room after school today. And all students must get their permission slips."

Drake thought that was what Mr. Zane would say.

"All permission slips should be signed. And they should be brought back to me tomorrow," Mr. Zane said.

Drake walked over to Mr. Zane's desk to help him look. If he didn't find them, the students would have to go by Mr. Zane's room after school. And Drake didn't want to do that.

Where were the missing permission slips? Did Mr. Zane forget where he had put them? But Drake didn't believe that.

Chapter 4

It was the same day. Drake walked into the lunchroom. He got his lunch. Then he looked for Jack.

Jack had his science class right before lunch. And Drake wanted to ask him about the permission slips.

Drake saw Logan. Logan was sitting with one of his girlfriends.

Then Drake saw Jack. Jack was at a table with Paige and Willow.

Drake walked over to the table and sat down with his friends.

"Did Mr. Zane find the permission slips, dude?" Drake asked.

"Yes. And boy is he upset," Jack said.

"Why? Where did he find them?" Drake asked.

"Yeah. Where did he find them?" Paige asked.

"Mr. Nash found them in a big trash can," Jack said.

Mr. Nash helped to clean the school. He also fixed things around the school.

"Why were the permission slips in the trash can?" Drake asked.

"Mr. Zane doesn't know why, Drake," Jack said.

"Mr. Zane should be happy now. He got the permission slips back. Now he won't have to run off more permission slips. So why is he still upset?" Drake asked.

"Someone spilled a lot of black paint into the trash can. And the paint got on the permission slips," Jack said.

"Why would someone dump black

paint into the trash can?" Paige asked.

"Maybe someone from the art class did it," Drake said.

"Maybe. But why?" Willow asked.

"To get rid of the paint," Drake said.

Paige said, "No one would get rid of paint that way, Drake."

"You don't know that, Paige. That could be why the paint was in the trash can," Drake said.

"Maybe someone didn't want Mr. Zane to pass out the permission slips. So that someone put the permission slips into the trash can. And then spilled the paint," Paige said.

"That's dumb," said Drake. "No one was trying to get rid of the permission slips."

"You never know. Maybe someone was trying to do that. I think we should try to find out who did it," Paige said.

"Who cares who spilled the paint? And who cares why they spilled it? We still have to go on the field trip," Drake said.

"You might have fun on the trip," Willow said.

"Yeah, dude. You might have fun on the trip," Jack said.

"Maybe. But I'll be late to football practice today. And the coach won't like that," Drake said.

"Why will you be late?" Willow asked.

"Yes, Drake. Why?" Paige asked.

"Mr. Zane said he'll run off more permission slips during his lunch. Then we have to go to his room after school," Drake said.

"I have Mr. Zane after lunch. So I can get you a permission slip. And I'll give it to you when you get home," Willow said.

"Will you get one for me, too, Willow?" Jack asked.

"Sure," Willow said.

"Get one for Logan, too. And I'll tell him," Drake said.

"Okay," Willow said.

Drake was glad Willow would get the permission slip for him. Now he wouldn't be late to football practice.

But he would still have to go on the field trip. There was no way he could miss it.

Chapter 5

The next day, Drake was in the lunchroom. He was at a table with Logan, Paige, and Willow.

Drake saw Jack walk quickly into the lunchroom.

Jack got his lunch. Then he came over to the table and sat down.

Jack said, "I have some news."

"What?" Drake asked.

"Yeah. What?" Logan asked.

"Mr. Zane is very upset," Jack said.

"Why? My entire class brought their permission slips back today. Did some of the students in your class forget their permission slips?" Drake asked.

Drake knew that would really upset Mr. Zane.

"No. Mr. Glenn came to see him," Jack said. Mr. Glenn was the principal.

"Why did Mr. Glenn see Mr. Zane?" Willow asked.

"Oh, I want to know, too," Paige said.

Jack said, "Mr. Glenn came about our field trip. He wanted to know why Mr. Zane had called off our field trip."

"Mr. Zane called off our field trip? That's great news," Drake said.

"I don't think it's great news, Drake," Willow said.

"I do," Logan said.

"Mr. Zane didn't call off the field trip," Jack said.

"Then why did Mr. Glenn think he did?" Paige asked.

"Yeah, Jack. Why?" Logan asked.

Jack said, "Someone called the bus office. The person said Mr. Zane told him to call. And he said Mr. Zane had called off the field trip. The person also said Mr. Zane wouldn't need buses next Friday either."

"Who called the bus office?" they all asked.

"Mr. Glenn didn't know," Jack said.

"It must have been someone in the school office," Willow said.

"Yeah. But who else would call?" Logan asked.

"Mr. Zane didn't call off the trip. So why did someone call the bus office? Why did the person say Mr. Zane had done that?" Drake asked.

"It must have been a mix-up. Maybe some other teacher called off a field trip. And the person in the bus office got mixed up," Willow said.

"Who else is going on a field trip?"

Drake asked.

No one knew about any other field trips. So no one had an answer for that.

The five ate for a few minutes. And they didn't talk.

Then Paige said, "Maybe the person in the bus office was right. Maybe someone did say Mr. Zane had called off the trip. Maybe that someone doesn't want Mr. Zane's classes to go on the trip."

"That's dumb, Paige," Logan said.

"Yeah, Paige. That's dumb. Why would someone do that?" Drake asked.

"I don't know. But I might be right about that," Paige said.

But Drake didn't think Paige could be right.

Drake didn't want to go on the trip. He knew some other students who didn't want to go either. But no one would try to stop the classes from going on the trip.

Chapter 6

It was the next Tuesday. Drake was in science class.

Class had started. And Mr. Zane was talking about their class work.

Mr. Glenn walked into the room. And Mr. Zane stopped talking.

"I'm sorry to bother your class, Mr. Zane. But I must talk to your students about something," Mr. Glenn said.

Why did Mr. Glenn want to talk to them? Was it about the field trip?

Mr. Glenn said, "Someone is playing jokes on Mr. Zane. And I want to know who it is."

Drake couldn't believe someone was playing jokes on Mr. Zane. Who would dare to do that?

"What kind of jokes?" Noah asked.

"Mr. Zane ran off some permission slips to your parents. Someone took those slips and threw them away. And then spilled paint on them," Mr. Glenn said.

"But that wasn't a joke. Someone must have done that by mistake," Noah said.

Mr. Glenn looked at Noah. Then Mr. Glenn said, "That's what I thought at first."

Why did Mr. Glenn change his mind about that?

Drake hoped Mr. Glenn would tell them what had happened.

Mr. Glenn looked at the other students in the class. He said, "Then someone called the bus office. They said Mr. Zane called off your field trip."

But the students already knew that. So why didn't Mr. Glenn talk to them about that last week?

Noah said, "I thought someone made a mistake. And the person got our trip mixed up with some other teacher's field trip."

Mr. Glenn looked at Noah again. "So did I," he said. "But someone called the bus office again. And said again that Mr. Zane had called off the trip."

That surprised Drake. "Why would someone do that twice?" he asked.

Mr. Glenn said, "I don't know the answer to that. But I do know all those things weren't mistakes."

Now Drake was sure they weren't mistakes either.

Mr. Glenn said, "I need to know who did those things. I need to know why the person did them. And I need to know before Friday."

"What if you don't find out before Friday?" Noah asked.

Drake wanted to know the same thing. But he didn't dare ask.

"Then I'll call off the field trip," Mr. Glenn said.

"Why?" Drake asked.

Mr. Glenn said, "I think the person is playing jokes on Mr. Zane. But I might be wrong. The person might want Mr. Zane's classes to stay here and not go on the trip."

Did that person want the science classes to stay at school?

"And the person might do something that would hurt someone," Mr. Glenn said.

Noah said, "You might not find out who did those things. And we can't go on the field trip. And that would be too bad."

But Noah didn't seem like he thought it was too bad.

And Drake didn't think it was too bad either. He didn't want to go on the trip. Maybe it would be okay some other day. But not on Friday.

Still, Drake hoped that Mr. Glenn found out who did those things.

But were they just jokes? Or were they something worse?

Chapter 7

Drake was glad when his lunchtime came. He wanted to talk to his friends about what Mr. Glenn said.

Drake hurried into the lunchroom. He got his lunch. Then he looked for his friends.

He saw Logan, Jack, Paige, Lin, and Willow at a table. Drake hurried over, and he sat down.

Drake said, "Mr. Glenn came by my science class today. And he talked to my class about the field trip."

"He came to my class," Logan said.

"The same for my class," Jack said.

"Why did he do that?" Paige asked.

"Yes, Drake. Why?" Willow asked.

"I want to know, too," Lin said.

Drake told the girls what Mr. Glenn had said.

Then Willow asked, "Who would want to play jokes on Mr. Zane?"

"I know a lot of people who want to do that," Logan said.

"So do I," Drake said.

"That's for sure," Jack said.

"But I don't know anyone who would dare do it," Drake said.

Paige said, "Maybe no one is playing jokes on Mr. Zane. Maybe someone doesn't want the classes to go on the field trip."

"But why?" Drake asked.

"I don't know why," Paige said.

"And who did those things? I don't want to go on the trip. But I wouldn't do something like that," Drake said.

"And I wouldn't either. That's for sure," Jack said.

"So who did them?" Logan asked.

No one had an answer for that.

The friends ate for a few minutes. And they didn't talk.

Then Lin stopped eating.

Paige asked, "What's wrong with you, Lin? Why did you stop eating your lunch?"

"Are you okay, Lin?" Willow asked.

At first, Lin didn't answer. Then Lin said, "I might know who did those things."

"Who?" the other five asked at the same time.

"I might be wrong. So I'm not sure I should say," Lin said.

"You should tell us, Lin," Willow said.

"Yeah, you should," Logan said.

"It might be Noah. But I don't know he did those things. So I might be wrong about him," Lin said.

"Noah? Why do you think it might be Noah?" Drake asked.

"Noah dates Hannah. And Hannah is in my science class," Lin said.

"What does that have to do with the field trip?" Drake asked.

Logan said, "Yeah, Lin. What does that have to do with the field trip? You don't have Mr. Zane for science."

"I heard Hannah talking to someone. She said Noah wants to stay out of school on Friday. He wants to go out of town," Lin said.

"Why?" Drake asked.

"Noah wants to watch his brother play in a football game this weekend. But his brother goes to a college out of state. And it'll take all day Friday to get there," Lin said.

"And Noah can't miss the trip. Or he would have to bring a doctor's note. And he couldn't do that," Drake said.

"I think Noah did those things. That's for sure," Jack said.

"We don't know for sure that Noah did those things. So you shouldn't say for sure that he did them," Willow said.

"I think Noah did those things," Paige said.

"So do I," Logan said.

"And I think one of us should tell Mr. Glenn," Paige said.

"I don't think we should do that. We don't know for sure that Noah did those things," Willow said.

"But we don't know what else Noah might do. And someone might get hurt," Paige said.

"Yeah, someone might get hurt," Drake said.

"Maybe we can prove Noah took the permission slips and made the calls. And then tell Mr. Glenn," Lin said.

"Maybe we can," Logan said.

"But how can we prove he did those things?" Willow asked.

No one had an answer for that.

Chapter 8

Drake and his friends were still at lunch. They all ate for a few minutes. And they didn't talk.

Then Willow said, "We need a plan."

"That's for sure," Jack said.

Lin said, "Drake is in science with Noah. So maybe Drake can talk to him. And maybe Noah will tell Drake he did those things."

Drake said, "I can talk to Noah. But he won't tell me he did them."

They ate for a few more minutes. And they didn't talk.

Then Paige said, "I have an idea."

"What?" the friends asked at the same time.

Paige said, "Drake can talk to Noah. And he can tell Noah that he doesn't want to go on the trip."

"How would that help us to find out?" Logan asked.

"Yeah, how?" Drake asked.

"Drake can tell Noah that he knows Noah did those things. He's glad Noah did them. Then Drake can thank Noah. And maybe Noah will tell Drake he did them," Paige said.

"That sounds like a plan to me. But I'm not sure it'll work," Drake said.

"But it might work," Willow said.

"Yes. It might work," Jack said.

"Hurry and finish your lunch, Drake. Then find Noah. And talk to him before lunch is over," Paige said.

"Yeah, dude," Logan said.

"And maybe Noah will tell you he did those things. And then you can tell Mr. Glenn," Paige said.

"Okay," Drake said.

But Drake still wasn't sure the plan would work. He quickly ate the rest of his lunch. Then he put his tray away.

Drake looked for Noah. Then he saw him. Noah sat at a table with Hannah.

Drake went over to their table.

"Okay for me to talk to you for a few minutes, dude? Just the two of us?" Drake asked.

"Sure," Noah said.

Hannah quickly got up from the table. She picked up her tray. Then she said, "I'll see you in class, Noah."

Hannah hurried away from the table.

Drake sat down at the table.

"What do you want to talk about?" Noah asked.

Drake didn't want to lie to Noah.

But someone was trying to get Mr. Zane to call off the trip. And Drake had to find out if it was Noah.

"I want to thank you," Drake said.

Noah seemed surprised. "For what?" he asked.

"For what you did," Drake said.

"What are you talking about, Drake?" Noah asked.

But Drake was sure Noah knew.

"You don't want our class to go on the field trip. So you dumped the permission slips into the trash. And you called the bus office," Drake said.

Noah didn't say anything.

Drake said, "And I'm glad you did. I have a game that night. And I don't want to go on a trip that day. So thanks."

Noah laughed. Then he said, "Okay. I did those things. But how did you find out?"

"I heard you want to go out of town. So you can go to your brother's football game," Drake said.

"Yeah," Noah said.

Noah had said he did those things. So Drake thought it was time for him to tell Noah the truth.

Drake said, "I'm going to tell you the truth, Noah. I don't like what you did. And I'm going to tell Mr. Glenn. Unless you want to tell him."

Noah seemed very mad.

"You can tell Mr. Glenn. But I won't tell him I did those things. And you can't prove I did," Noah said.

Drake said, "I'll still tell Mr. Glenn. And I think he'll be able to prove you did them."

Drake didn't think Noah would go on the trip on Friday. But now Drake was sure his science class would go. And he was sure he would have to go, too.

But maybe he would have fun on the trip after all.